The Checkup

by Helen Oxenbury

Dial Books for Young Readers

E. P. Dutton, Inc. New York

Mommy took me to the doctor
for a checkup.
"You'll have to wait your turn,"
the nurse said.
The waiting room smelled funny.
I opened the window.

Nobody wanted to talk to me.
"Maybe they're not feeling well,"
Mommy whispered.

"Who's next?" the doctor asked.
"Come on, it's our turn," said Mommy.
"I want to go home," I said.

"Well, young man, shall we listen
to your chest?"
I sat on Mommy's lap.
"See," Mommy said, "it doesn't hurt."

"If you do what the doctor says,
   I'll buy you something on the way home,"
Mommy whispered.

"Let's go home now, Mommy," I said.
The doctor fell off his chair.

"Call the nurse!" said the doctor.
"I'm so sorry," said Mommy.

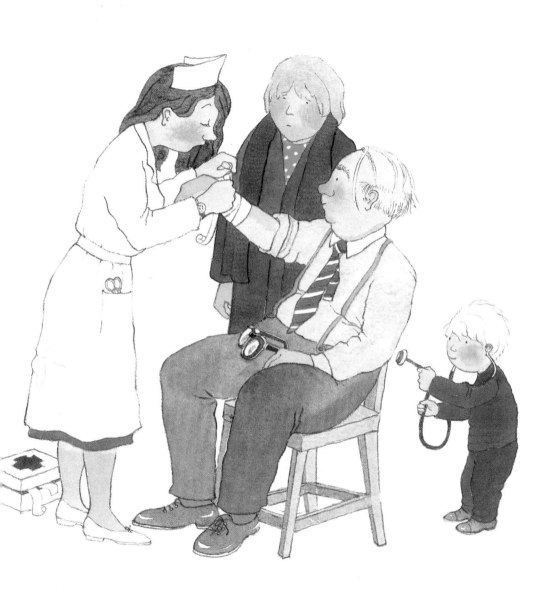

"He seems normal enough,"
  the doctor said. "I won't have to see
  him for another year, I hope."
"I like the doctor," I said.
"I think he's really nice."